WITHDRAWN

To the little kid across the street,
who saw it first. —A. B.

This one is for Bubbie,
who believed in me first,
and still does, thankfully. —N. L.

Library of Congress Cataloging-in-Publication Data available.

ISBN 978-1-4521-6336-9

Manufactured in China.

Design by Sara Gillingham Studio.
Typeset in Colby.
The illustrations in this book were rendered digitally.

10 9 8 7 6 5 4 3 2

Chronicle Books LLC
680 Second Street
San Francisco, California 94107

Chronicle Books—we see things differently.
Become part of our community at www.chroniclekids.com.

WHAT JOHN MARCO SAW

by **ANNIE BARROWS**

illustrated by **NANCY LEMON**

chronicle books · san francisco

John Marco had two brothers and two sisters.

They were all bigger than he was.
They were all louder than he was.

They all talked a lot.

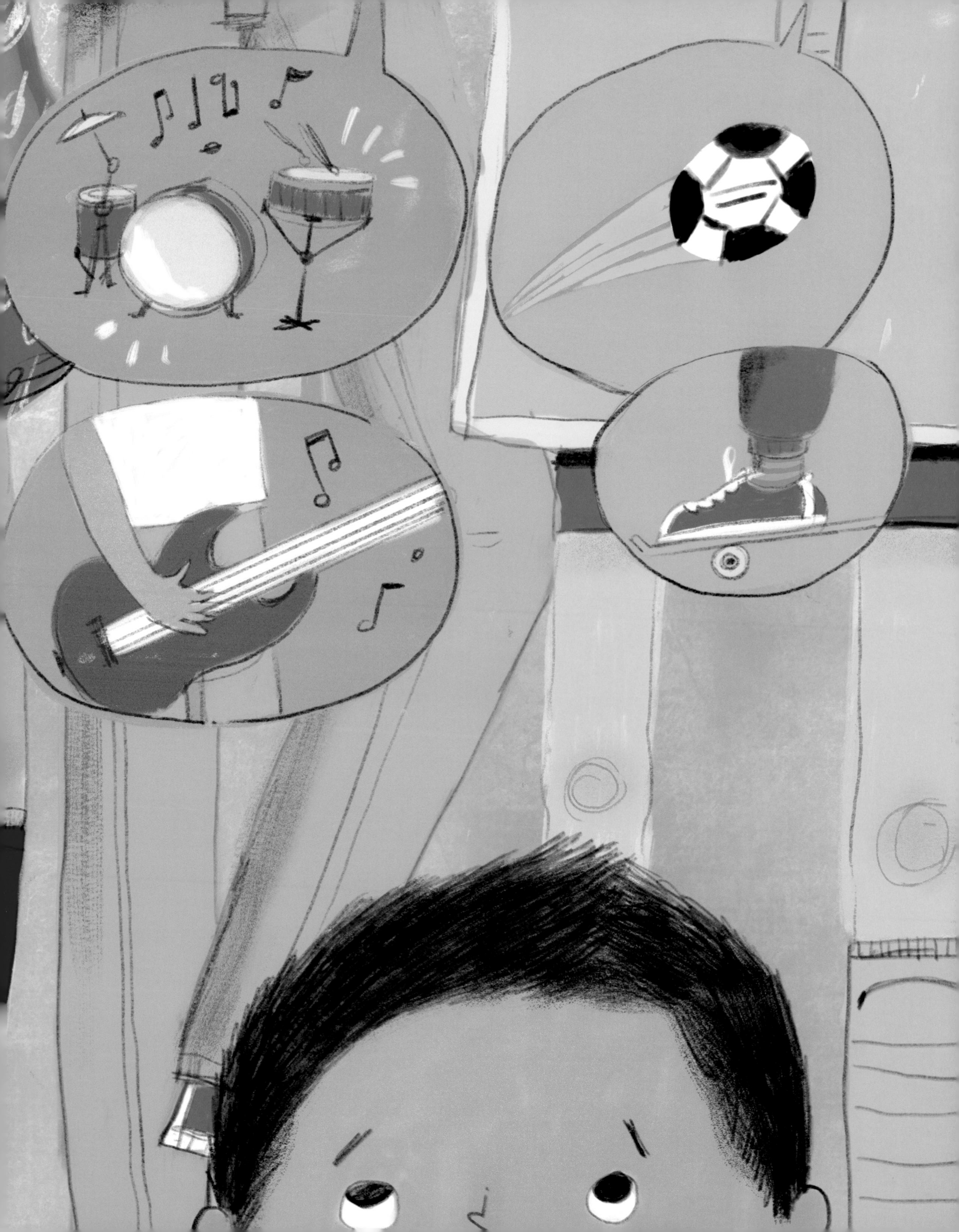

When John Marco had
something to say, like:

“Today I saw this big green
grasshopper in the yard.
Its eyes were all black and bulgy. . . .

And it was eating a
piece of grass, and
I could hear it chew,
like this, *ch-ch-ch*,”

nobody listened.

John Marco decided to try his neighbor, Mr. Jordy.
Mr. Jordy liked to sit on his porch and read his newspaper.
Also, he liked to whistle.

John Marco said,
"I dug a hole in the mud. . . .

And I found a bunch of worms
and also a rock that had a white line in it,
and I think it's a fossil.

You want to see?"

Mr. Jordy did not want to see.

John Marco decided
to try his mom.

His mom was very busy.
She was doing four things at once.

John Marco said,
“A big old orange cat
came into the yard,

and her stomach was
almost dragging on the ground
she was so fat. . . .

She lay down in the grass,
and I thought she might like some water,
so I put some in a bowl and set it down,
and she looked at it but she didn't drink. . . .

And she let me sit right next to her,
and she closed her eyes
and went *prrr-rrup.*"

John Marco went outside.
He sat on the front step.

After a while, he got up.

He stood on the grass and looked
at the tree in the middle of the yard.
He looked hard at the tree.

It was falling down.

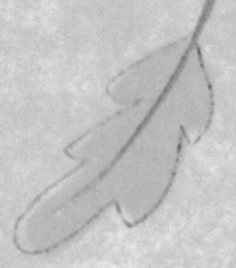

It was falling down very slowly,
but it was definitely falling down.

John Marco said,
"The tree in the front yard
is falling down."

Nobody listened.

John Marco said,
"The tree
in the front yard
is falling down!"

His brothers and sisters
came outside.

“The tree in the front yard
is falling down,”
explained John Marco.

Mr. Jordy looked
through the leaves.
“What tree?”
he asked.

“THE TREE IN THE FRONT YARD IS FALLING DOWN!”

yelled John Marco.

John Marco's mom came outside.

"Trees don't just fall down," she said.

"This one does,"
said John Marco.

click
?!?

8
WINNER

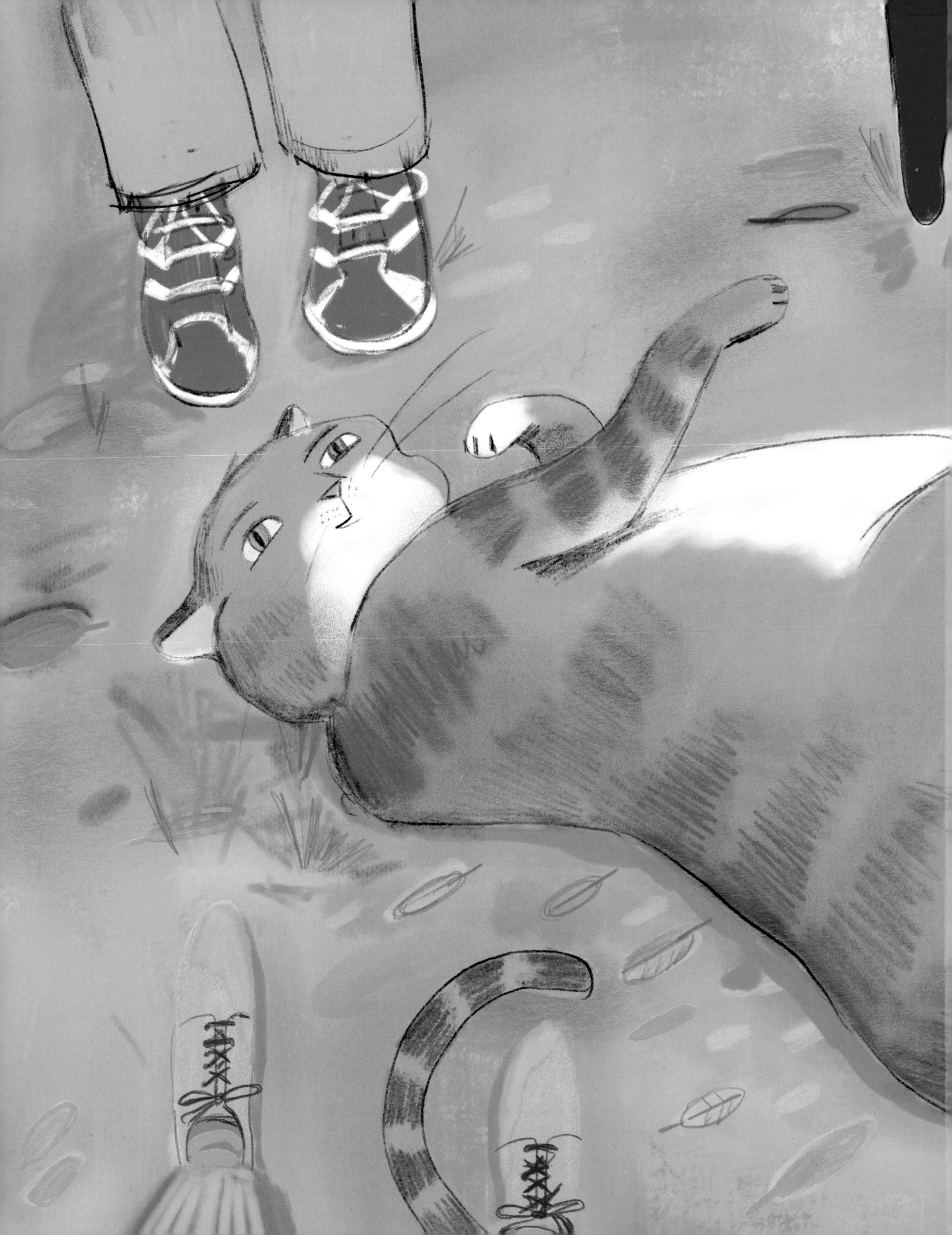

The fat old orange cat rolled over.

"You people should
pay more attention," she said.
"Like John Marco does."

“Hey! Look!”